MW00946449

Santa's Patch

Written by Ronda Neilson
Illustrated by Tatiana Hubich

SANTA'S WORKSHOP

Snow flurries fell, and the night sky was clear.
It was the eve before Christmas, the best time of year.
Santa's workshop is quiet, tidy, and neat,
The toy making's finished, all orders complete.

Santa checked off his list, then checked it once more,

Confirming everything the children wished for.

"It's time," Santa boomed. "Let's load up the sleigh.

Harness the reindeer, and let's get on our way!"

Poppy
Raja
Jane
Porter
Kenn
Brookles
Kade
Coco
Marki
Honey
Cal
Shauna
Max
Walker
Doc
Brady
TC
Kade J
Kora

Soap

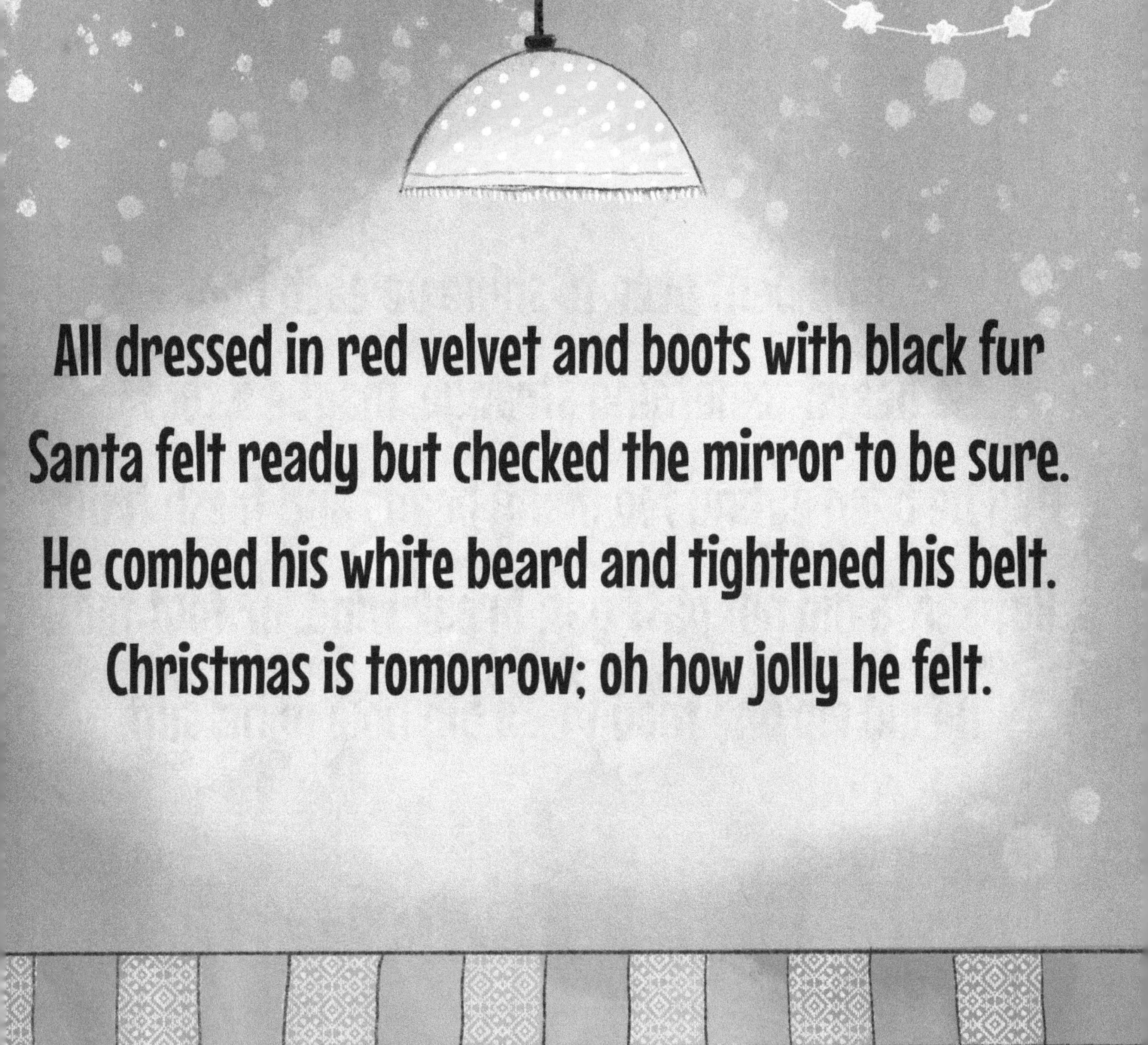

All dressed in red velvet and boots with black fur
Santa felt ready but checked the mirror to be sure.
He combed his white beard and tightened his belt.
Christmas is tomorrow; oh how jolly he felt.

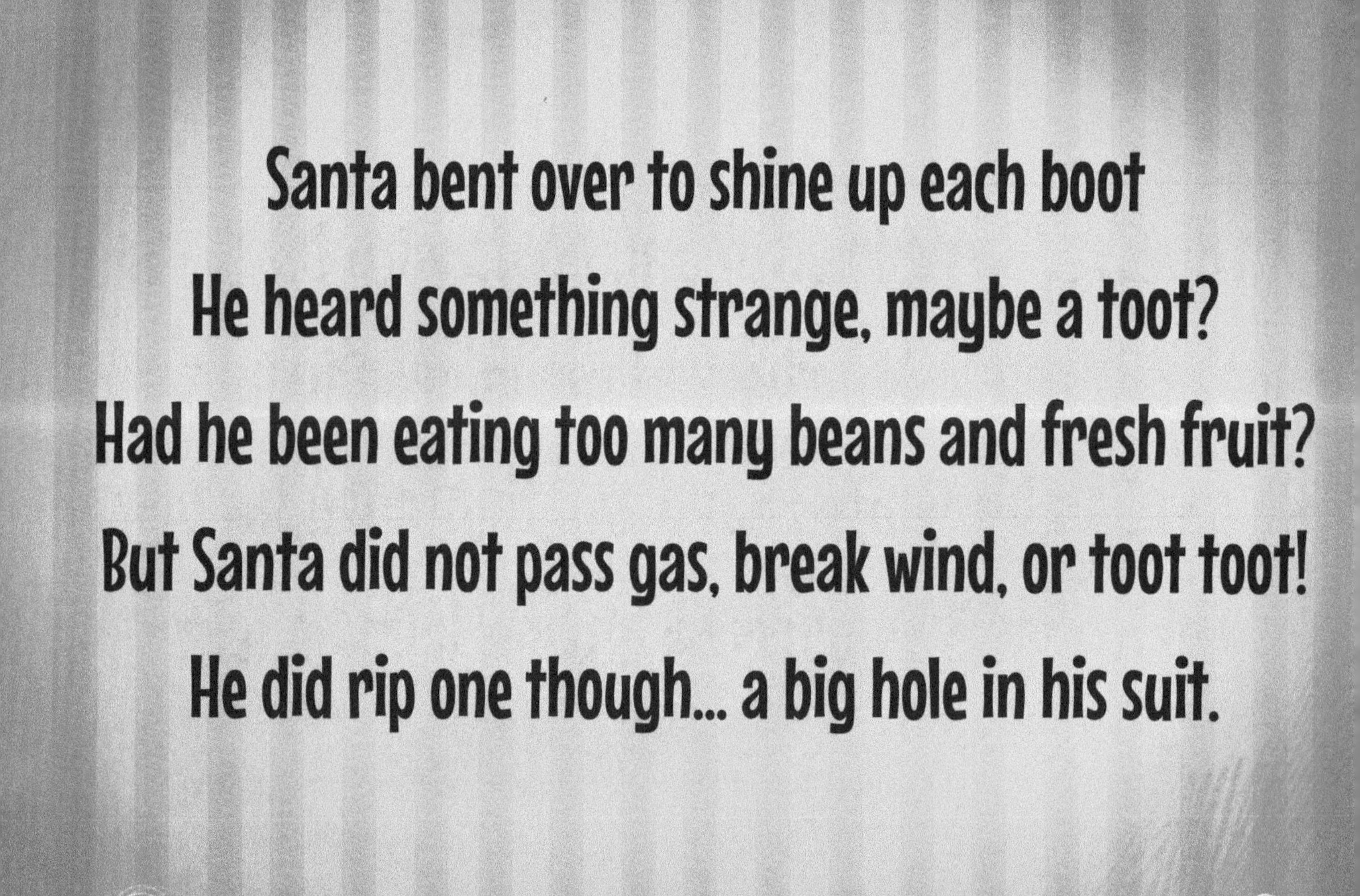

Santa bent over to shine up each boot
He heard something strange, maybe a toot?
Had he been eating too many beans and fresh fruit?
But Santa did not pass gas, break wind, or toot toot!
He did rip one though... a big hole in his suit.

Turning around, he saw the big tear.

A rip in his pants let in the cold air.

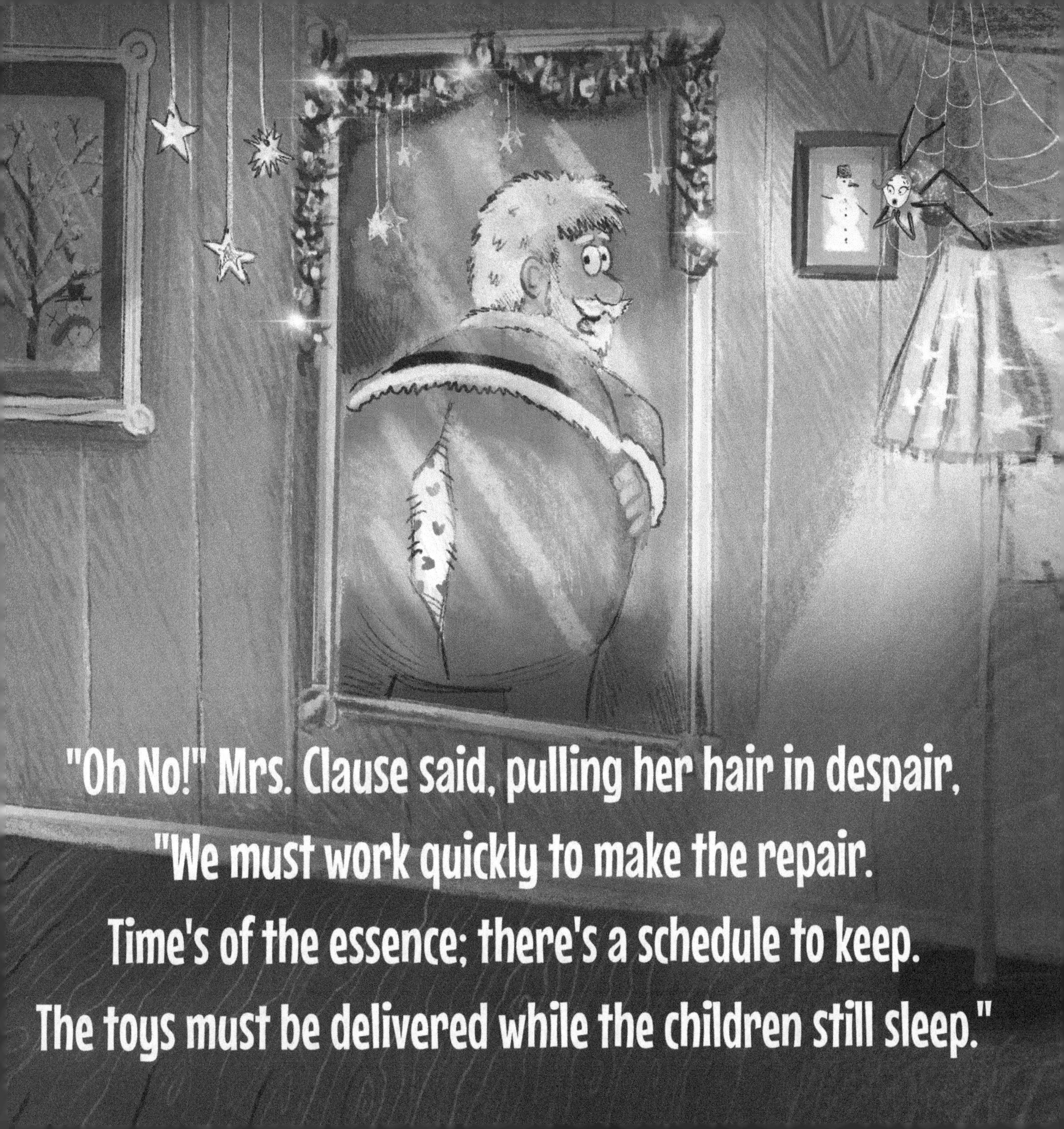
"Oh No!" Mrs. Clause said, pulling her hair in despair,
"We must work quickly to make the repair.
Time's of the essence; there's a schedule to keep.
The toys must be delivered while the children still sleep."

Something must be done; Santa's briefs were in view!
But the elves had the fix, and they rushed in with glue.
Squeezing the bottle, the goo blooped out with a push,
Then they dolloped the glue, on Santa's round tush.
Santa's pants didn't hold; the Gooey Glue made a mess.
"What do we do now?" Santa asked in distress.

Glue

Santa had to get going; the night would be long.
Mrs. Clause said, "Try packing tape; it's sticky and strong!"
When she tore off a piece, the tape turned to a clump
Mrs. Clause did her best to cover up his torn rump.
The tape didn't hold, and Santa was anxious to go
But he couldn't head out with his undies on show!

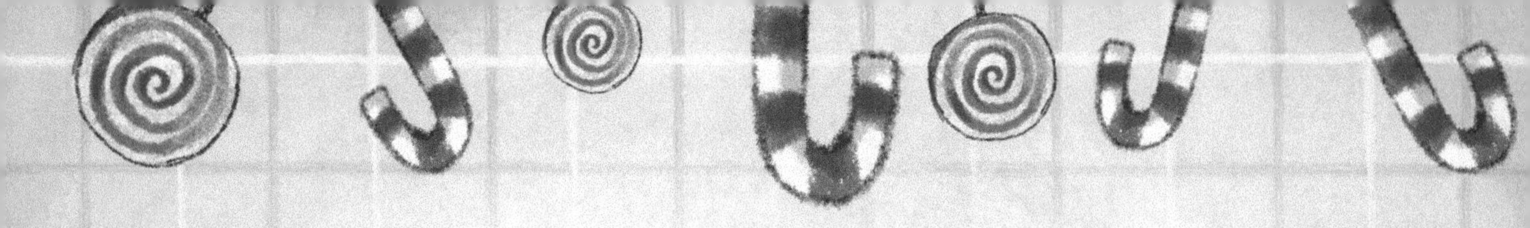

Mrs. Clause racked her brain, for something to fuse -
Some type of an adhesive, oh what could she use?
Then looking around, a thought came to mind
She saw what was needed to cover his behind
Christmas is a time for all types of treats:
Lollipops, candy canes, and anything sweet,
Sugar plum berries and Santa's favorite - Bubble Gum.
Maybe yummy candy, could cover Santa's bum?

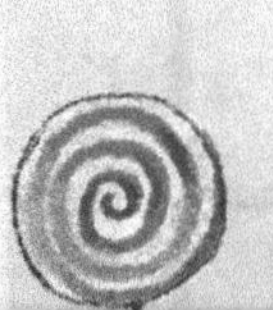

"That's it!" Mrs. Clause thought - Bubble Gum we should try.

"It's sticky and grippy," and she began to apply.

She started with gum, then sugar sweets on his seat

Hoping the candies, their grip they would keep.

"This is not working," Santa said with a doubt.

After all that she tried, Santa's briefs still stuck out.

Mrs. Clause searched the workshop, for the best resolution.

Perhaps a nice patch would be the solution?

She needed some fabric - something soft would be nice

She pulled off her apron. "This will have to suffice."

She measured the rip and the size of the hole
Covering up Santa's boxers was her ultimate goal.
Mrs. Clause trimmed her apron, a heart shape she did cut -
a beautifully designed patch, to cover Santa's butt.
She had her gold needle, but no thread to repair
the rip in Santa's pants, that showed his derriere.

The Spider viewed the trouble that Santa was in.

With a desire to help, she started to spin.

A shiny web she spun, of silver and gold.

It dazzled and glistened, so strong and so bold.

Oh, how it sparkled, like tinsel on the tree.

Her web made with magic; a Christmas spider was she.

With a patch made with love, and newly spun fiber
Mrs. Clause went to work, with help from the Spider.
Santa started giggling, as she started to sew.
Her sewing tickled; Santa laughed. “Ho! Ho! Ho!”
"Hold still!" Mrs. Clause said, "Please stop squirming and bending."
Her hands quickly sewed, and she smiled while mending.

When Mrs. Clause finished, Santa started to cheer.
Santa's patch was like artwork, and covered his rear.
The patchwork was brilliant, so sleek and unique.
He hugged Mrs. Clause, then kissed her rosy cheek.
Santa was proud of the patch on his britches
Now he was ready, to fulfill Christmas wishes.

Santa praised the Spider, and her neat magic silk,
Then he finished his cookies and last gulp of milk.
Registration and passport, he wouldn't forget,
Along with his pilot license, Santa was set.
Then looking at his watch, and checking the hour,
Santa climbed in his sleigh, and amped up the power.

Pilot
license

Mapping his route, for every time zone
Santa now realized - he wasn't alone.
There on his boot, was a special surprise
Hiding in the fur, was the Spider in disguise.
Santa delighted, and with a twinkle in his eye,
He welcomes the Spider, along for the ride.

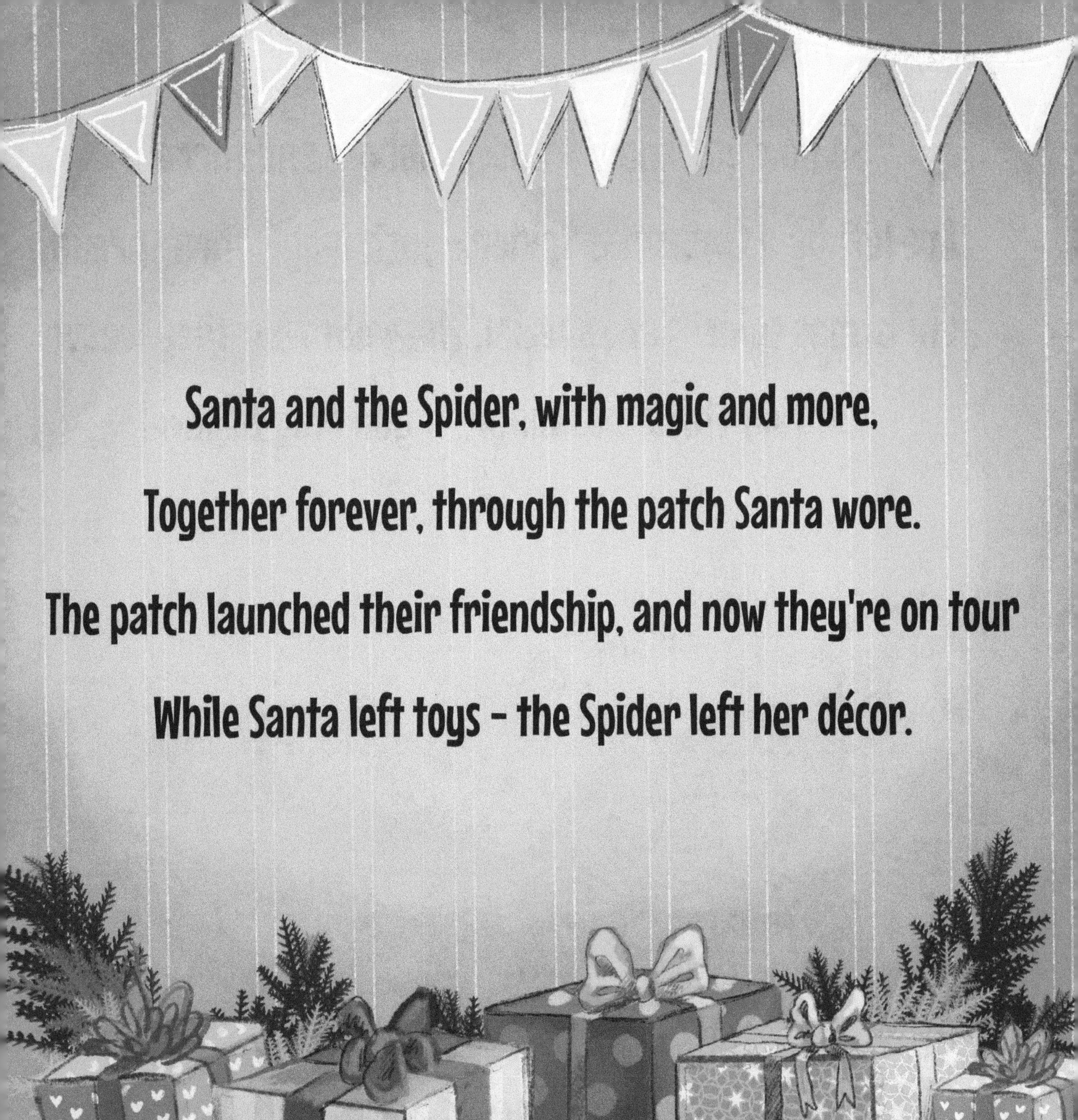

Santa and the Spider, with magic and more,

Together forever, through the patch Santa wore.

The patch launched their friendship, and now they're on tour

While Santa left toys – the Spider left her décor.

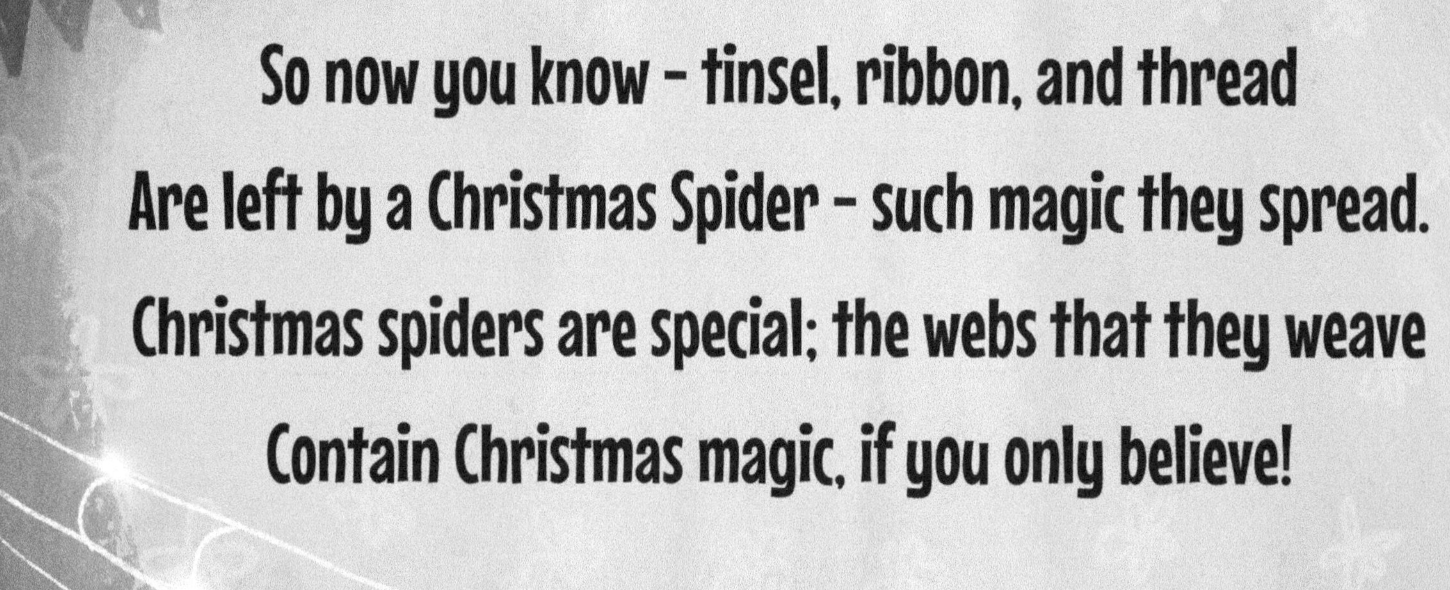

So now you know - tinsel, ribbon, and thread
Are left by a Christmas Spider - such magic they spread.
Christmas spiders are special; the webs that they weave
Contain Christmas magic, if you only believe!

ABOUT THE AUTHOR

Ronda Neilson, the debut author of "Santa's Patch," was born and raised in the beautiful foothills of Utah. Santa's Patch began with 4th-grade Ronda, and now decades later, with years of revisions, her Christmas story is finally in print. She has a passion for education and is the third generation of music educators. She is a proud mother of five children and two grandchildren and plans to have as many grandchildren as possible in her home.

Ronda is creative, adventurous, and has an infectious personality. She is full of entrepreneurship spirit as she owns many businesses and enjoys working with nonprofit organizations. She loves helping people achieve their personal, educational, and professional objectives. Ronda hopes this story will delight readers as her goal is to make others happy.

Ronda and her husband reside in Southern Utah and enjoy the beauty of the landscape and the outdoor adventures it provides.

ABOUT THE ILLUSTRATOR

Tatsiana Gubisch is a creative artist and art educator living in Minks, Belarus. She is passionate about creating children's book illustrations and developing characters and portraits in various art styles and designs. Tatsiana's talented ability to make a story come alive with her eye for detail makes every book she illustrates a treasure for all. Tatiana hopes you will enjoy her beautiful illustrations and the story of Santa's Patch.

ISBN: 978-1-387-47834-7

CPSIA information can be obtained
at www.ICGtesting.com
Printed in the USA
LVHW061135281222
735792LV00036B/777

9 781387 478347